It's Fun to Learn

A Tree for Me

One day, Owl heard DRIP-DROP-DRIP! His roof had sprung a leak!

"Oh, dear," said Owl, hurrying to get a pot. "This will never do."

Later, when Owl went to empty the pot, he couldn't move. His feet were stuck to the floor in a puddle of sticky tree sap.

"My house is falling apart!" he cried. "It's time to look for a new tree."

"Hiya, Beak Lips!" called Tigger, bouncing up for a visit. "Whatcha doing?"

"I've decided to move," Owl explained. "And I'm making a list of the things I want for my new house. I'll need a tall tree with a sturdy trunk and lots of leafy branches in just the right spot."

"Hey, I'll help ya!" cried Tigger. "Finding tree houses is what tiggers do best!"
So the two friends walked through the Wood looking at different trees. Soon they
found Piglet, who was out collecting haycorns.

"Owl's lookin' for a new tree to call home," Tigger explained.

"Oh," said Piglet. "What about this one?" He pointed to a tree right behind him.

"Noperoo," said Tigger, shaking his head. "That one's too skinnyish."

"Hey, fellas...whaddaya think of this one?" asked Tigger, bouncing up to the treetop. "These leaves look exackatackly like stars."

"Sweet sassafras!" cried Owl. "I daresay this tree's leaves look just like mittens! And who wants a mitten tree for a home?"

"Absoposilutely!" Tigger agreed. "Let's keep lookin'!"

Suddenly Tigger cried out, "Ahem and ahoom! This tree's all abloom. Well, go on. Try her on for size."

Owl flew over to take a closer look. "Oh, dear," said Owl. "These—achoo!—flowers—achoo!—tickle my beak—achooooo!"

Recovering, Owl turned to Tigger and said, "Now look here, Tigger, I can certainly pick my own—"

But Tigger had already bounced on to the next tree.

"Hey, this is the firstest tree I've everest seen with all its branchedy branches upside down at the bottom," he cried.

"Those aren't branches," cried Owl. "They're tree roots."

"Oh, dear!" exclaimed Piglet. "I hear a buzzing sound!"

Pooh happened to be nearby, staring up at a beehive.

"Oh, dear!" said Piglet. "There are bees in those trees!"

"Alas," Owl added sadly, "yet another taken tree."

Owl and his friends walked on. They soon found the perfect tree near Eeyore's house of sticks.

"It's a good tree," Eeyore said, "if you like a lot of noise."

"No, no, no," Owl insisted. "A woodpecker already lives in this tree."

"Don't worry, my feathered friend," said Tigger. "We just gotta find you another one. We've got plenty to choose from around here:

There're leafy trees that touch the sky...

And blossomin' bloomers...me, oh, my!

There're fruit-filled ones a mile high,

And baby trees that you can try!"

"Yes," Owl agreed. "And I'd like to pick my own particular kind, if you don't mind!"

"Sometimes a fruit tree comes in handy," said Eeyore, "when you're in the mood for a fruity snack." BONK!

But Owl wanted a quiet tree, not a tree with falling apples.

"Well, this oak tree is my kind of tree," said Piglet. "See all those lovely haycorns growing on it?"

"I dunno, Piglet Ol' Pal," said Tigger, bouncing up to take a closer look. "Those squirrels look awfully suspisherous to me. I say they're hidin' thing-a-ma-bobs in there."

"Those are nuts they're storing for the winter," said Owl. "This tree is taken, too."

"Don't give up, now," said Tigger, pointing to a giant maple tree. "I'm gonna find you the perfeckty tree. Lookee! Here's a good one for swingin'! Next to bouncin', swingin' is what tiggers do best. Hoo-hoo-hoo!"

"A swing is simply not on my list," said Owl. "What I need is a place to put my cozy chair and all my books and family albums."

"What about this tree?" suggested Piglet. But Owl could see a possum family already lived there.

"Hey! Lookee here! A sideways tree!" cried Tigger. "But you wouldn't have much room to spread your wings, would ya?"

"You don't seem to understand," Owl said impatiently. "I need a tree that's fit for me."

"Aw," said Tigger. "Don't be such a stick in the mud. Let's have a good bouncety bounce in this big ol' pile of leaves. That'll take your mind off your troubles!"

But after Tigger insisted on bouncing through many leaf piles, the sun began to set. Owl was disappointed as he headed home with his friends.

"Maybe we'll find your new tree on the way," said Piglet.

"Or tomorrow," added Pooh.

"Tomorrow will do," added Eeyore. "Just hope it doesn't rain tonight."

Suddenly Owl stopped in front of a big tree. "Yes, yes, yes!" he cried. "This tree is tall with a good sturdy trunk, and it's in a positively perfect spot. Why, I think I've found my new home!"

"Hoo-hoo-hoo!" Tigger cried. "You've not only found your new home, Beak Lips, you found your *old* one. Thanks to me, of course!"

"All it needs is a little fixing up," offered Piglet.

"And we'll help you," said Pooh.

"Tree-mendous idea," said Tigger. "After all...that's what friends are for!"

Fun to Learn Activity

I say, we saw quite a few different kinds of trees while searching for my new home. There were leafy ones that touched the sky and "blossoming bloomers," too! Can you go back through my story and describe the trees we found? What made them special?

Look in your own backyard. What kind of trees do you see?